PUFFIN BOOKS

Jack Sweettooth the 73rd

Malorie Blackman is an ex computer-programmer who now writes full time. She has had a number of jobs, including database manager, systems programmer, receptionist and shop assistant. As a database manager she travelled extensively to places such as Toronto, Geneva, New York and Dallas.

Not So Stupid!, her first collection of short stories was a Selected Twenty title for Feminist Book Fortnight, 1991. Since then she has published over fifteen books, including *Hacker*, which won both the W. H. Smith Mind-Boggling Books Award and the *Young Telegraph*/Gimme 5 Children's Book of the Year Award in 1994, and the *Girl Wonder* series. She has contributed to numerous anthologies for both adults and children. She lives in London with her partner and several pets, including a frog, some bears, an owl, a haggis, a whale and a penguin – all stuffed toys!

Some other books by Malorie Blackman

GIRL WONDER AND THE TERRIFIC
  TWINS
GIRL WONDER TO THE RESCUE
WHIZZIWIG

MALORIE BLACKMAN

Jack Sweettooth the 73rd

Illustrated by Patrice Aggs

PUFFIN BOOKS

For Neil with love
And for my sister, Wendy

PUFFIN BOOKS

Published by the Penguin Group
Penguin Books Ltd, 27 Wrights Lane, London W8 5TZ, England
Penguin Books USA Inc., 375 Hudson Street, New York, New York 10014, USA
Penguin Books Australia Ltd, Ringwood, Victoria, Australia
Penguin Books Canada Ltd, 10 Alcorn Avenue, Toronto, Ontario, Canada M4V 3B2
Penguin Books (NZ) Ltd, 182–190 Wairau Road, Auckland 10, New Zealand

Penguin Books Ltd, Registered Offices: Harmondsworth, Middlesex, England

First published by Viking 1995
Published in Puffin Books 1997
10 9 8 7 6 5 4 3

Filmset in Palatino

Made and printed in England by Clays Ltd, St Ives plc

Contents

1
Blame the Mouse!

Eight o'clock

Hi! I'm Jackson Winstanley Sweettooth the seventy-third – or Jack for short – at your service!

I live with Mr Bailey, Mrs Bailey, Matthew and Shani, in this house.

Mr Bailey likes me. "As long as he doesn't run over my feet!"

Shani is very fond of me. "Jack is great fun!"

Matthew loves me. "Jack is my best friend."

Mrs Bailey . . . isn't too keen! "Keep that smelly, horrible creature away from me!"

Never mind! It's Shani's birthday today and I intend to be extra-super-duper helpful. I shall prove to Mrs Bailey that she's all wrong about me!

Eight fifteen

"AARRGH! No one move. No one *breathe*! The ruby has fallen out of my eternity ring. AARRGH!" shrieked Mrs Bailey.

"I've been telling you for ages to go and get your ring fixed, dear," sighed Mr Bailey.

Mrs Bailey fell to her knees and started sweeping her hands back and forth over the grey carpet.

"Come on, you lot! No breakfast until my ruby is found!"

"But that could take ages," said Matthew, his stomach rumbling.

"Then the sooner you start helping, the sooner we can all eat," said Mrs Bailey.

Matthew walked over to me. "Come on, Jack," he whispered. "If anyone can find Mum's ruby, you can."

He let me out of my cage and put me on the carpet. Here was my chance to shine! This was my chance to show Mrs Bailey that I, Jackson Winstanley Sweettooth the seventy-third, could be *useful*!

I was soon on the job! Sniffing here and searching there and keeping my eyes peeled. I ran everywhere – over the videos and under the sofa and between the books on the floor, until . . .

"Eeek! Who let that nasty, disgusting creature out of its cage?" screamed Mrs Bailey.

"I thought Jack could help us," said Matthew.

"Help us! HELP US! I bet that . . . that . . . mouse has *swallowed* my ruby by now!" said Mrs Bailey.

"But, Mum – " Shani protested.

"Jack wouldn't do that," said Matthew.

"Dear, I really think –" began Mr Bailey.

But Mrs Bailey wasn't having any of it.

"Matthew, put that animal back in its cage. We're all going round to the vet's,"

said Mrs Bailey. "I just know that rodent
has eaten my ruby!"

So we all left the house and got into
the car and off we went to the vet's.

Eight forty-five

"Has Jack had any breakfast this
morning?" The vet scratched her head.

"None of us has had any breakfast this morning," muttered Mr Bailey.

Mrs Bailey elbowed her husband in the ribs.

"No," said Matthew, "Jack hasn't eaten anything since yesterday evening."

"Good. That makes it easier. If Jack has swallowed the ruby from your mum's eternity ring it will show up nicely on the X-rays," said the vet.

I was put under a huge machine which clanged and rumbled and whirled. There was a sudden loud buzzing sound, but it didn't hurt at all – and then it was all over.

Five minutes later, the vet came out into the waiting-room, where we were all sitting. Guess what?

"Sorry, Mrs Bailey," said the vet. "I don't know where your ruby is, but it's *not* in Jack's stomach."

Huh! I could've told you that! I thought.

So we all drove home again.

Nine fifteen

"I guess my ruby has gone for good," Mrs Bailey sighed unhappily once we were home.

"Never mind, dear," said Mr Bailey, giving her a hug. "I'm sure it will turn up."

"Mum, what about my birthday party?" said Shani. "All my friends will be here at three."

"Never mind your birthday party! What about breakfast?" said Matthew.

"OK! OK!" said Mr Bailey. "I'll make breakfast. You two go and make your beds and tidy your rooms until I call you."

Off went Matthew, huffing and puffing and mumbling about his breakfast. I was pretty hungry myself!

Mr Bailey made bacon and beans on toast for breakfast and Matthew sneaked me some. It was most excellently tasty!

After breakfast, Mrs Bailey started making Shani's birthday cake.

Meanwhile Shani and Matthew made

all kinds of sandwiches: banana and bacon, ham and mustard, cheese and raspberry jam, strawberries and sugar, egg and pickle. Then they put lots of different kinds of cakes and mini Swiss rolls and pizza slices on lots of different-sized plates.

And I watched the whole thing from Matthew's shirt pocket. It all looked yumptious! Matthew even managed to slip me a bit of a strawberry and sugar sandwich. Scrumptious!

"Come on then, Shani, Matthew. Time to go to the hairdressers," said Mrs Bailey. She turned to her husband. "Paul, can you keep an eye on the birthday cake and take it out of the oven when it's cooked?"

"Of course, dear," smiled Mr Bailey. He hates going to the hairdressers!

"Shani, you can have your hair styled, and, Matthew, you can have yours cut," said Mrs Bailey.

So off we went.

When we reached the hairdressing salon, it was jam-packed solid full of people. Almost every sink had someone's head leant backwards over it. Each hairdryer had someone sitting under it. We had to wait a while, but then Shani was taken off by one

23

hairdresser and Matthew was led away by another. It wasn't too bad, until . . .

A woman under a hairdryer started the commotion.

"EEEK! A MOUSE!" she screamed. "AARRGH! HELP!"

The man beside her flung his newspaper in the air and leaped out of his chair. But he forgot that the hairdryer was still over his head. His head hit the inside of the hairdryer with a loud THWACK! Then the man slid back down into his seat. I think he knocked himself out.

Meanwhile, a man wearing perm rods leaped on to his chair, yelling, "A MOUSE! A MOUSE!"

By this time, all the other grown-ups were joining in. They were dashing here, there and everywhere. They fell over each other, yelling and screaming. Some

24

leaped over chairs in their hurry to get out of the salon. One woman fainted and dropped to the floor like a stone.

It was worse than sports day at Shani and Matthew's school!

Another woman ran into the loo and locked the door, screaming, "Call the police! Call an ambulance! Call my husband! AARRGH! A MOUSE!"

Shani came rushing over. "Matthew, you idiot! You didn't let Jack go, did you?"

But before Matthew could answer, Mrs Bailey appeared to stand in front of Shani and Matthew, her hands folded across her chest. Lightning bolts flashed from her eyes.

"I want a few words with you, Matthew!" she said stonily.

"I didn't do it, Mum," Matthew said immediately. "Honest I didn't."

"Why did you let that dreadful mouse loose?" Mrs Bailey asked. "That wasn't very funny."

"Mum, I didn't –" Matthew started.

"Of all the daft, pea-brained –" began Mrs Bailey.

"But, Mum, it couldn't have been Jack," Matthew said. "Jack's in –"

"Not another word," Mrs Bailey interrupted.

"Oh dear! I'm so sorry, Mrs Bailey. I really must apologize." One of the hairdressers came running up.

Mrs Bailey looked surprised. "Apologize? For what, Sam?"

Sam hopped from foot to foot, looking very embarrassed. "Er . . . it's just that

26

. . . all week they've been knocking down that old cinema a few doors down. And the place was infested with hundreds of mice. They've been running through all the shops in the high street. I'm sorry if they scared you. We are trying our best to get rid of them."

"Mice! You mean this salon is full of mice?" Mrs Bailey stared.

"That's what I was trying to tell you, Mum," said Matthew. "It couldn't have been Jack. Jack is still in my pocket. See!"

"Oh!" said Mrs Bailey. "Matthew, I'm sorry, I didn't let you explain."

And then Mrs Bailey gave me a really strange look.

We stayed in the hairdressers until Shani had had her hair styled and Matthew had got his hair cut.

Then Mrs Bailey drove us home. And I didn't see a single mouse the entire time.

What a shame! I would've liked to say hello to some of my cousins!

One fifteen

There it sat, on the kitchen table. It was perfect! It was stupendous! It was the best, the most wonderful, the most rumptious, the most delectably delicious birthday cake Mrs Bailey had ever made.

"I'm brilliant!" smiled Mrs Bailey.

"I was the one who took it out of the oven," said Mr Bailey. "That's where all the skill was needed!"

When the cake had cooled, Mrs Bailey poured *tons* of chocolate icing all over it.

"Oh, Jack! Look at that!" Matthew breathed. "I bet . . . I bet, if I had a teeny-tiny, itsy-bitsy little bit, no one would ever know!"

Uh-oh! I thought. Uh-oh! And my whiskers started to quiver – a sure sign of TROUBLE!

Two o'clock

"Mum! MUM! Look at this!" Shani yelled from the kitchen.

We all came running.

"Look!" Shani pointed to her birthday cake. And there, in the side of it, was a hole . . .

"Matthew, have you been letting that repulsive, revolting rodent nibble at your sister's cake?" Mrs Bailey glared at me with beady eyes.

I went hot – from the end of my tail to the tips of my whiskers.

"I'm waiting, Matthew," said Mrs Bailey.

"I . . . I . . ." Matthew spluttered.

And as Mrs Bailey continued to scowl at me, I could feel myself getting hotter and hotter.

31

"Wait a minute, Mum," said Shani.
She prodded at the hole in the cake with
her fork. "There's a whole lot more
missing from this cake than just a hole!
And someone's tried to disguise it by
smearing over the chocolate icing to
cover it up!"

Shani prodded the cake from the top,
as well as the side. "There's a whole slice
gone!" she said.

Mrs Bailey turned to Matthew. "As far

as I know, mice can't cut *slices* out of
birthday cakes!" she said.

"I . . . I . . ." Matthew stammered.

"You greedy, toad-faced gannet!"
Shani pouted. "It was *you* who cut a slice
out of my birthday cake. And there was
Mum blaming poor Jack!"

"Matthew? Did you take some of your
sister's cake?" asked Mrs Bailey.

"Yes, Mum." Matthew hung his head.

I glanced up at Mrs Bailey. There! You

see! I didn't do it! I thought.

And Mrs Bailey watched me, a strange expression on her face.

Two thirty

Matthew's Mum and Dad discussed whether or not Matthew should be allowed at his sister's party.

"It's up to you, Shani," they decided.

"Oh, all right then. You can come, Matthew. But if you take so much as a crumb off this table before my party starts . . ."

"Thanks, Shani!" Matthew grinned gratefully.

"I mean it, Matthew!"

"I won't. I promise," Matthew said quickly.

"Hmm!" said Mr Bailey.

"Hmm!" said Mrs Bailey.

"Hmm!" said Shani. "You'd better not!"

Still in disgrace, Matthew was sent to wash his hands and face before the party.

"Oh dear!" Matthew sighed to me. "I shouldn't have done it, but I couldn't resist it! That cake looked so tempting!"

I burrowed down into Matthew's shirt pocket. I'd had enough of being blamed for everything for one day!

Matthew closed the bathroom door. He fished me out of his pocket and let me run over the bathroom floor, the way he always does.

"It wasn't my fault," Matthew muttered. "That cake was calling to me, *teasing* me."

I ran back and forth and up and down, stretching my legs.

And then I saw a strange thing. A
gleaming, glinting, strange thing,
winking at me from the tiny space
between the bath-tub and the bathroom
cupboard. I nudged my nose closer to it
and there it was! Mrs Bailey's ruby!

I squeezed myself into the teeny-tiny space and started to nose out the ruby.

"What are you up to, Jack?" asked Matthew.

"Squeeek!" I said. "Squeeeek!"

And I carried on pushing at the ruby with my nose until it was out in the open.

"Squeeeeek!" I said.

Matthew picked me up and put me back in his shirt pocket. He bent over to see what I'd been doing. Then he saw it.

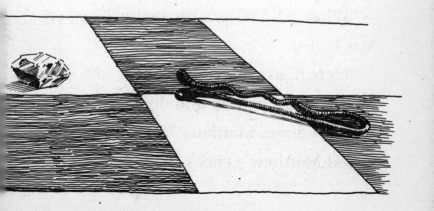

His mum's gleaming, glinting ruby. He
snatched it up.

"Mum! MUM!" Matthew shouted.

Mrs Bailey came running. So did Shani
and Mr Bailey.

"What is it? What's the matter?" asked
Mrs Bailey.

"Here it is! Your ruby! Here it is!"
Matthew jumped up and down.

"Well done, Matthew!" Mrs Bailey
kissed Matthew's cheek.

Matthew looked at his mum. Then he took me out of his pocket "I . . . I didn't do it, Mum," said Matthew. "Jack found it. He pushed it out from between the cupboard and the bath-tub."

Mrs Bailey gave me another strange look. A long, slow, very strange look. Then she did something she'd *never* done before. Very slowly, very carefully, she picked me up and sat me in the palm of her hand.

"Thank you, Jack," smiled Mrs Bailey, using my proper name for the first time ever. "I've blamed you for everything that went wrong today. I think I've always been too hard on you and I'm really sorry. I'll try to make it up to you."

And she did!

Three o'clock

I got some of *everything* from Shani's birthday party – and Mrs Bailey made me my very own birthday cake, even though it wasn't my birthday.

Double rumptious-yumptious-scrumptious!

It's so nice to be appreciated!

2
This House isn't Big Enough for Both of Us!

Beauregard Battersby-Bunge

The sun was shining, birds were singing, the sky was a deep blue with not a single cloud to spoil the view. We were all out in the garden. Mr and Mrs Bailey sat on the garden bench, kissing and cuddling and canoodling – yuk! Shani sat on the swing reading her latest book and Matthew sat on the grass playing with one of those pocket video games. I ran back and forth and up and down on the grass by Matthew's feet, just enjoying myself. I stopped to look up at the sky. It was such a wonderfully beautiful day.

Nothing can go wrong on a day like today, I thought.

But I was mistaken.

Without warning, my whiskers began to quiver and to shiver and to shake. I looked around. Everything looked normal . . . but something, somewhere

was not right. I moved closer to Matthew's shoe, just to be on the safe side.

And then I saw him. Beauregard Battersby-Bunge! The ginger cat from next door.

Threats and Promises

"Squeeeek!" I almost jumped out of my skin at the sight of him.

Beau started grinning at me – a horrible, slinky, sly grin that sent a shuddery-juddery feeling right down my spine to the tip-top of my tail. He was sitting on the fence, half hidden by some of the low-lying branches of our pear tree.

"Purrr!" he said softly. "Hello, Jackson. You arrre looking . . . fat!"

I clambered up on to Matthew's foot. I wasn't taking any chances.

"Sleek and glossy and wonderrrfully *fat*!" Beau licked his lips.

I swallowed hard. "Don't even *think* of trying to eat me, Beau," I squeaked. "Matthew and Shani would stop you before you even got close to me."

"Ah, but Matthew and Shani won't be arrround all the time. One day it'll be just you and me . . . and then it'll be just me," Beau threatened.

"No chance, you sneaky, skulking, overgrown carrot!" I said, puffing myself up until I was as big as I could get.

"We'll see," purred Beau. "We'll see."

And with that he jumped down off the fence and started slinking towards me. I squeaked and squealed and screeched at the top of my voice until Matthew looked up from his video game to see what was

wrong with me. Then he saw Beau.

"Hello, Beau." Matthew smiled at the cat. "Have you come to watch me play this game?"

And all the time Beau was slinking closer and closer. When Beau was less than half a metre away he sat down on the ground, never taking his eyes off me.

"Matthew, you'd better put Jack in your pocket before Beau pounces," Mrs Bailey warned.

Thank you, Mrs Bailey. Thank you! Thank you! I thought gratefully.

What was Matthew playing at? Was he just going to leave me sitting there to become Beau's mid-morning snack? Matthew picked me up and put me in his shirt pocket. I sat absolutely still and I didn't wriggle once. All right, I admit it! I was sulking. If I didn't know any better I would think that Matthew wanted me to be eaten!

"Don't worry, Jackson," Beau said.
"I'll get you yet – that's a prrromise."

And suddenly the day wasn't quite as wonderful any more.

Mr Morton's Accident

"Hi, Mr and Mrs Bailey. Hello, Shani and Matthew." Mr Morton from next door popped his head above the garden fence. I raised my head above Matthew's pocket and had a look around. Beau was still sitting close to Matthew, watching me. He was getting on my nerves!

"Hello, Mr Morton," said Mr Bailey. "What're you up to?"

"Just cutting back my lilac tree," said Mr Morton. "Oh, so there you are, Beau. I wondered what had happened to you."

"He's been watching Jackson, our

mouse, for ages now," said Shani.

"He's trying to make friends," said Mr Morton.

It's just as well I wasn't eating something when Mr Morton said that, otherwise I would've choked, for sure!

"I see my cat is more interested in your garden than his lunch," smiled Mr Morton. "Beau, your food is in the kitchen whenever you're ready."

Beau didn't move. Mr Morton winked at Matthew.

"Beau always did know his own mind," laughed Mr Morton.

And with that he started climbing up his step-ladder to get to the branches that were sticking out the most on his lilac tree. Keeping one eye on Beau, I watched Mr Morton snip away at some of the branches with his shears. He struggled to cut a particularly thick branch right above his head. Then he stepped back to get a better look at the branch – only he forgot he was on a step-ladder and he went crashing backwards to land with a great thud on the ground.

We'll Look After Him

Everyone in the garden sprang up at once and ran over to the fence. But we were all too late. Mr Morton lay on the ground, clutching at his arm.

"Mr Morton, are you all right?" asked Mrs Bailey.

"I think . . . I think I've broken my arm," groaned Mr Morton.

"Shani, go inside and call for an ambulance," said Mr Bailey.

Shani ran into the house. Mr Bailey climbed over the fence and tried to make

Mr Morton more comfortable but he kept groaning, and even from my position within Matthew's pocket I could see that he was in a great deal of pain. The ambulance crew confirmed what Mr Morton had said.

"Yep! You've definitely broken your arm, mate!" said the ambulance woman.

"We'll take you to the hospital and get you fixed up in no time," said the ambulance man.

They tried to lay him out on a stretcher.

"I can't go to hospital," Mr Morton protested. "What about Beau? What about my cat?"

"Don't worry about Beau, Mr Morton," said Mrs Bailey. "We'll look after him."

And with those few words, my heart sank. I turned to look at Beau. His smile was blinding now. And I knew I was in deep, *deep* trouble.

Beau Tries His Luck

Mr and Mrs Bailey decided to visit Mr
Morton in hospital. I squeaked and
squeaked up at Matthew to take me with
him, but Mrs Bailey put her foot down.

"Matthew, you can't take Jackson to
the hospital and that's final," she said.

So, reluctantly, Matthew put me in my
cage. Mr Bailey brought Beau into the
house and fed him some tuna-fish.

It took less than five minutes for me to realize that the house wasn't big enough for both me and Beauregard Battersby-Bunge! One of us would have to go – and I had no intention of going anywhere.

I'll say this for Beau – he was smart. Whenever anyone was around, he'd lie absolutely still and pretend to be asleep or pining for Mr Morton. But the moment it was just him and me in the room, he'd jump up to stand in front of

my cage and then he'd try to get his claws in between the bars. Suddenly the metal bars of my cage looked as substantial as wet paper.

Matthew charged down the stairs. Beau only just had time to jump down before he got spotted next to my cage.

"We'll be back soon," Matthew told me. "So try to get along with each other."

And with that Mr and Mrs Bailey, Shani and Matthew left the house.

Beau jumped up beside my cage before the front door was even shut. I crouched in the corner of my cage, as far away from him as I could get.

"Go away, you rotten cat. Go away!" I hissed at him.

"Come overrr herrre!" Beau whispered. "Then I'll go away."

I mean, did I really look that stupid!

But when Beau couldn't get to me, he started trying other things. This time he stood by the side of my cage and tried to force it away from the wall. And slowly but surely Beau kept nudging and shoving and swiping at my cage, until at last the cage began to move towards the edge of the table.

"I'm going to get you," purred Beau. His tongue came out to lick his lips.

I swallowed hard. Now my cage was seesawing up and down at the edge of the table. I looked down. The carpet looked like it was kilometres away. One more push from Beau's claw . . .

Then everything happened at once. Beau swiped at the cage and it teetered one way, tottered the other and then – WHOOSH! – it sailed through the air to land with a CRASH! on the carpet. My cage door sprang open because of the impact. I didn't wait another second. I sprang out of the cage and raced for the sofa. I felt a cold breeze waft over my back. My blood froze as I realized that the breeze wasn't a breeze at all, but was Beauregard Battersby-Bunge's claws missing me by millimetres! I didn't stop. I raced for the sofa as if my life depended on it – which it did! And I made it – just in time. Beau ploughed into the sofa above me the second I escaped under it.

"I hope you've broken your head," I squeaked out.

"You just wait, you rrrotten rrrodent!" Beau howled.

He tried to swipe underneath the sofa, but the opening was too small for him to get even one claw under it.

"Come out, Jackson. I was only joking," wheedled Beau.

"Very funny. Excuse me whilst I just split my fur laughing!" I replied. "But if you don't mind, I'll crease up laughing from *under* the sofa."

"Come out this second or you'll be sorry," Beau screamed at me.

"If I come out, I'll be a lot sorrier than I am now," I said. "So thanks, but no thanks."

"Rrright then. I'm going away now.

You'rrre not worrrth all this fuss," said
Beau.

As if I'd fall for an old trick like that!
What an insult to my intelligence! I
moved even further back. Then suddenly
I felt a bang against the sofa. Then
another. And another. Beau was trying
to move the sofa to get to me. What a
twit! As if a cat like that could move a
huge, heavy sofa. But then I felt the sofa

give a little shake and move just a teeny-tiny bit.

I was in big trouble – again!

Saved by Scatty Shani!

"Honestly, Shani, you're so scatty," said Mrs Bailey, opening the front door.

"Squeek! SQUEEEK!" I said, as loudly as I could.

"You'd forget your head if it wasn't screwed on," smiled Mrs Bailey as they both walked into the house.

"Uh-oh!" said Beau.

He went to sit in the middle of the carpet and miaowed loudly.

"What on earth. . . ?" Mrs Bailey came into the living-room.

"Jackson! Beau's eaten Jackson," Shani whispered, horrified.

"Squeek!" I said again. And I emerged from underneath the sofa to nudge at Shani's leg.

When Beau saw that he miaowed louder still.

Mrs Bailey saw what was going on straight away, in spite of Beau trying to look all sweet and cute and innocent in the middle of the room.

"You wicked, wicked cat," said Mrs Bailey, picking him up. "So that's what you've been up to whilst we went to visit Mr Morton, is it?"

"It's lucky I forgot the box of chocolates we were taking to Mr Morton, or Jackson could've been Beau's lunch by now," said Shani.

Mrs Jackson went out into the back garden and put Beau down on the ground.

"You, sir, are no longer welcome in

our house," said Mrs Bailey. "I'll prepare all your food in Mr Morton's house until he gets out of hospital, but you're not eating anything in our house – and especially not Jackson."

That's right! You tell him! I thought, from the safety of Shani's hand.

Beau licked one paw, then the other. Then he slunk away into Mr Morton's garden without saying a word.

And I, for one, wasn't sorry to see him go! No I was not!

3
A Friend of My Own

Sitting and Watching

"Jack, why don't you come out and have a run round the garden?" Shani said to me.

I sat in my cage and watched the birds singing and listened to the dogs barking in our neighbour's garden, all through my open cage door. I sighed, then sighed again.

"It's all right, Jack. Beau is at the vet's," said Matthew.

Even the news that Beauregard, next door's pesky cat, was at the vet's didn't cheer me up.

"Something's definitely wrong with Jackson, Mum," Shani said. "He hasn't been eating his food. He doesn't race round and round in his wheel. He won't even stretch his legs in the garden."

And do you know something? Shani was absolutely right. I *was* pining for something. But – what made matters worse – I had no idea what!

Matthew Does His Best Friend a Favour

The next day, I lay in my cage, my head on my front paws, and did absolutely *nothing*. I didn't eat, I didn't sleep, I didn't exercise. I watched my fur grow! Mrs Bailey came home from work at lunchtime. She sat in front of my cage and frowned and frowned at me.

"Come on, Jack. You can't mope about for ever you know," she said.

I sighed.

Mrs Bailey tried feeding me all my favourite things, like strawberries dipped in sugar and bananas dipped in honey, but I wasn't hungry.

"I give up on you, Jack, I really do," Mrs Bailey said at last. And off she went to make her family's dinner.

Soon Matthew came home. And guess what? He was carrying a cage – just like mine.

"Mum, I hope you don't mind, but I told Ben that we'd look after his mouse whilst his family are on holiday," said Matthew.

Mrs Bailey frowned. "Oh, Matthew, you should have spoken to me first," she said at last.

"I was only doing my best friend a favour. Does that mean we can't look after Blossom?" Matthew said, dismayed.

"Blossom?" asked Mrs Bailey.

Matthew held up the cage he'd just brought home with the mouse in. "This is Blossom," he said.

"When do Ben and his family go on holiday?" Mrs Bailey asked, moving towards the phone.

Matthew glanced down at his watch. "They've already gone! At two o'clock this afternoon!"

"Over two hours ago," smiled Mrs Bailey ruefully. "In that case, it would seem as if Blossom and I are stuck with each other."

"I'll put Blossom's cage next to Jack's," said Matthew. "They should get along just fine. There must be all kinds of mousey things that they can talk about."

So Matthew did just that.

From the moment Blossom's cage was put next to mine, I hated her! She took one look at me and gave a loud sniff as if she thought she was too good for me.

"Hello. I'm Blossom de Blo Blossom the first," she said, introducing herself.

"Jackson Winstanley Sweettooth the seventy-third – at your service," I said, standing up.

"The seventy-third?" she sniffed loudly. "My gracious!"

"I come from a long line of Sweettooths," I said. "Besides, what kind of name is Blossom de Blo Blossom?"

I only said that because she didn't like my name.

"It's the only name I've got," she told me.

"Huh!" I lay back down. I decided that
Blossom de Blo Blossom wasn't worth
getting up for. She was so stuck-up, with
her sniff-sniffing and her "My gracious!"

Which was a shame really, because she was the prettiest mouse I'd seen in a long, long time.

"So what's it like living here then?" she asked.

I sighed. It was obvious she wasn't going to take the hint and leave me alone.

"It's OK, I suppose," I sighed. "It gets a bit boring sometimes though. Same old thing, day in, day out."

"I was just thinking that about the Clarksons," said Blossom. "I must admit, when I knew Ben and his family were going on holiday I was quite glad when I found out I couldn't go with them. At last! I thought. Now I can meet Jackson Sweettooth."

I stood up again. "You did? I mean, you *did*?"

"Of course. Matthew told Ben all about

you and then Ben told me," explained Blossom.

"Then why did you sniff when I told you my name, as if I wasn't good enough?" I asked.

"My gracious! Did I sniff?" Blossom asked.

I nodded.

"If I did sniff, it's because I've got a cold and for no other reason," sniffed Blossom.

I went hot all over. "Oh dear. I . . . er . . . think I rather jumped to conclusions," I said. " You sniffed and I thought you didn't like me."

"Not like you!" Blossom was astounded. "Why, this is the greatest moment of my life!"

And from that time on I knew Blossom and I were going to be the very best of friends.

What My Problem Was

For the next week, Blossom and I ate and played together every single day. It was wonderful. And I slowly realized why I hadn't been eating and why I'd been feeling so poorly. Do you know what my problem was? I was lonely. I was lonely for some other mouse company, for a friend of my own.

Matthew and Shani put our cages together so that my door opened on to Blossom's cage and Blossom's cage opened on to mine. We ran round and round in our wheels together, having wheel races, or we'd sit and talk and talk – until by the end of the week, I'd made up my mind.

"Blossom de Blo Blossom," I said, "will you marry me?"

"Jackson Sweettooth the seventy-third," Blossom replied, "I thought you'd never ask!"

So we had a kiss and got married.

But the next day, when I woke up, Blossom de Blo Blossom had disappeared.

The Blossom Mystery

All kinds of horrible thoughts ran through my head. What if Beauregard Battersby-Bunge had eaten Blossom? What if she'd got buried by accident when Mrs Bailey was planting her petunias? What if . . . ? What if . . . ? I gnawed at my cage door until Matthew saw me.

"What's the matter, Jack?" he asked, putting the cage on the carpet.

I watched as Matthew opened the cage door, but before he could put his hand in

to pick me up, I was away. I ran under
his hand and scarpered across the carpet.
I had to find Blossom. I chased over the
living-room, then out into the front
room, then I ran upstairs, darting
between Mr Bailey's legs and avoiding
Matthew's swooping hands.

"Matthew, will you please keep that mouse under control," said Mr Bailey crossly, once he'd regained his balance.

"Sorry, Dad. I don't know what's got into him –" Matthew began.

I didn't wait to hear any more. I ran into Shani's bedroom.

"Eek!" Shani jumped on her bed.

I was the one who should have been afraid. Shani had on one of those cucumber and avocado face-packs. If I hadn't been so frightened about Blossom I would have had the fright of my life!

"It's only Jack," Matthew told his sister.

"I know that," said Shani, annoyed. She got down off her bed. "He startled me, that's all. I wasn't expecting him to come tearing into my bedroom."

I tore out again. After a quick look around it was obvious that Blossom wasn't with Shani. I ran into Matthew's bedroom, then into Mr and Mrs Bailey's. No Blossom. Then I ran back downstairs, with Matthew, Shani and Mr Bailey chasing behind me. Still no Blossom. Mrs Bailey came out of the kitchen.

"What on earth is going on?"

"It's Jack. He's upset about something," said Shani.

Mrs Bailey stood in front of the kitchen, her hands on her hips, her legs apart.

"Jackson, behave yourself. Ben Clarkson and his family came back from their holiday yesterday, so if you're looking for Blossom, that's where she is," said Mrs Bailey.

I came skidding to a halt, followed by Matthew, Shani and Mr Bailey.

Blossom had gone. And I hadn't even had a chance to say goodbye.

The Family Is Worried

Matthew picked me up and put me back in my cage. I lay down, staring at my paws, feeling worse than before Blossom had arrived. For the rest of the day I didn't even twitch a whisker, I didn't make a single squeak. Blossom was my very best mouse friend – she was my wife – and she'd gone away. Would I ever see her again?

Mr and Mrs Bailey and Shani and Matthew tiptoed around me all day. I

didn't care. I hardly noticed them. All I
could think about was Blossom de Blo
Blossom and how much I missed her.
And how lonely I was. And it was much
worse than before, because now I *knew*
how lonely I was. Mr Bailey was on the
phone for most of the morning. He kept
giving me strange looks as he spoke to
the person at the other end. I didn't care.
I didn't care about anything.

The doorbell rang. I still didn't bother to move. But then I saw Ben walk in carrying a mouse cage. And in the cage – yes! – it was Blossom. I stood up and squeaked my head off. So did she!

"I'm sorry, Jack, but they took me away whilst I was still asleep," said

Blossom. "I lay in my cage all day and decided I wasn't going to bat an eyelid until I saw you again."

"I'd decided the same thing," I told her happily.

"That's the first peep we've heard out of her all day," said Mr Clarkson, Ben's dad.

"It's the same with Jack," said Mrs Bailey. "It is good to hear him back to normal."

"So now, we'd better decide what we're going to do to keep them that way," said Mr Clarkson. And he and Mr and Mrs Bailey disappeared out of the room after putting down our cages.

Blossom and I nudged and snooked each other through the cage bars after they'd put her cage next to mine.

"We mustn't let them separate us again," said Blossom.

"Absolutely not,' I agreed.

But what could we do to stop them?

"We could run away," said Blossom.

"We have to be practical, dear," I said. "If Beau, the cat from next door, doesn't get us, then the first hungry owl flying around at night will."

Being a mouse means keeping a constant lookout!

"At least we'd be together," said Blossom.

Which was true!

But just then, Mr Clarkson and Mr and Mrs Bailey came back into the room.

"Jack, Blossom, we think we've reached a compromise," said Mr Bailey.

"That means they've come to an agreement that we'll all be able to settle for," Matthew whispered to me.

"During the week, Jack will stay with the Baileys and Blossom will stay with us," said Mr Clarkson.

"But we'll take it in turns to keep both of you at the weekends," said Mr Bailey.

"So for the first weekend, Ben will keep both Blossom and Jack," explained Mrs Bailey. "And the following weekend, it will be our turn to keep both the mice, and so on."

"So we'll only see each other at the weekends," said Blossom.

"Well, that's better than never seeing each other at all," I pointed out.

So we quickly discussed it. Then Blossom nodded her head and so did I.

"I'm glad that's settled," said Mrs Bailey. "Now, perhaps things can get back to normal around here."

"But things are *never* normal around here," said Shani and Matthew.

"You can't argue with that, dear," said Mr Bailey.

I looked at Blossom and she looked at me. We'd be together – every single weekend, we'd be together. Now *that* was more like it.

We twiddled and mingled whiskers! Until I realized that everyone was watching.

They all started laughing. And do you know something? I didn't even mind!

Also in Young Puffin

GIRL WONDER'S
WINTER ADVENTURES

Malorie Blackman

"You three are going to drive me bonkers."

Whether dressing up for Hallowe'en, building a snowman or carol singing, Maxine and her twin brothers have lots of fun. But things don't always turn out quite as expected, and the fun usually leads to TROUBLE for the mischievous trio!

GIRL WONDER
AND THE
TERRIFIC TWINS

Malorie Blackman

"OK, Terrific Twins, I have a plan."

When Maxine has a plan, you can be sure
that it involves her twin brothers Antony
and Edward. You can also be sure that it
involves – TROUBLE!

From rescuing Syrup the cat to cooling
people down at the local swimming pool, no
problem is too big for Girl Wonder and the
Terrific Twins. The trouble is, things never
seem to go according to plan.

'. . . sparkling stories'
– *Children's Books of the Year*

Also in Young Puffin

THE Hodgeheg

Dick King-Smith

Max is a hedgehog who becomes a hodgeheg, who becomes a hero!

The hedgehog family of Number 5A are a happy bunch, but they dream of reaching the Park. Unfortunately, a very busy road lies between them and their goal and no one has found a way to cross it in safety. No one, that is, until the determined young Max decides to solve the problem once and for all...

Also in Young Puffin

SEPTIMOUSE, BIG CHEESE!

Ann Jungman

**"Big, big people in a trice,
Be as small as little mice."**

As the seventh son of a seventh son,
Septimouse has amazing magical powers.
When little big person Katie's dad loses his job,
Septimouse has a brilliant plan. He shrinks
big, big person Mum and big, big person Dad,
and takes them through the mouse hole behind
the fridge! There they see the magnificent
mouse cheese factory Septimouse has created.
And from little cheeses big cheeses soon begin
to grow, and Dad gets a new job.

A funny book for
little big people
everywhere!

The Swoose

Dick King-Smith

"Are you feather-brained?" said the vole. "No, I'm Fitzherbert."

Fitzherbert is confused. With his oversized feet and snaky neck, he is shunned by the other goslings. Then his mother reveals that he is a rare breed of bird indeed – the offspring of her romantic liaison with a dashing white swan. With stars in his eyes, Fitzherbert sets off in search of his father and discovers fame beyond the farmyard in the household of the Queen of England herself!

'Other writers who put words into animals' mouths are outclassed'
– *The Times Educational Supplement*

'Judy Brown's enchanting black and white illustrations capture the spirit of both swoose and sovereign'
– *Independent on Sunday*

Also in Young Puffin

THE MIND-BOGGLING ADVENTURES OF NORMAN THORMAN

Lorna Kent

"This is it," he said to himself. "I'm really going to be on TV."

Until a large book falls on his head, Norman Thorman is a very normal, responsible boy. But while recovering in hospital, Norman discovers that something quite extraordinary has happened to him. He has developed a most unusual talent.

Two enormously entertaining stories about the lovable but accident-prone Norman Thorman, together for the first time in one volume.

Chosen by children as the Pick of the Year for the Federation of Children's Book Groups.

READ MORE IN PUFFIN

For children of all ages, Puffin represents quality and variety – the very best in publishing today around the world.

For complete information about books available from Puffin – and Penguin – and how to order them, contact us at the appropriate address below. Please note that for copyright reasons the selection of books varies from country to country.

On the worlwide web: www.puffin.co.uk

In the United Kingdom: Please write to *Dept. EP, Penguin Books Ltd, Bath Road, Harmondsworth, West Drayton, Middlesex UB7 ODA*

In the United States: Please write to *Consumer Sales, Penguin USA, P.O. Box 999, Dept. 17109, Bergenfield, New Jersey 07621-0120*. VISA and MasterCard holders call 1-800-253-6476 to order Penguin titles

In Canada: Please write to *Penguin Books Canada Ltd, 10 Alcorn Avenue, Suite 300, Toronto, Ontario M4V 3B2*

In Australia: Please write to *Penguin Books Australia Ltd, P.O. Box 257, Ringwood, Victoria 3134*

In New Zealand: Please write to *Penguin Books (NZ) Ltd, Private Bag 102902, North Shore Mail Centre, Auckland 10*

In India: Please write to *Penguin Books India Pvt Ltd, 706 Eros Apartments, 56 Nehru Place, New Delhi 110 019*

In the Netherlands: Please write to *Penguin Books Netherlands bv, Postbus 3507, NL-1001 AH Amsterdam*

In Germany: Please write to *Penguin Books Deutschland GmbH, Metzlerstrasse 26, 60594 Frankfurt am Main*

In Spain: Please write to *Penguin Books S. A., Bravo Murillo 19, 1° B, 28015 Madrid*

In Italy: Please write to *Penguin Italia s.r.l., Via Felice Casati 20, I–20124 Milano*

In France: Please write to *Penguin France S. A., 17 rue Lejeune, F–31000 Toulouse*

In Japan: Please write to *Penguin Books Japan, Ishikiribashi Building, 2–5–4, Suido, Bunkyo-ku, Tokyo 112*

In South Africa: Please write to *Longman Penguin Southern Africa (Pty) Ltd, Private Bag X08, Bertsham 2013*